First Facts®

U.S. NATIONAL PARKS FIELD GUIDES

GREAT SMOKY MOUNTAINS NATIONAL PARK

by Joanne Mattern

I0821562

PEBBLE
a capstone imprint

First Facts Books are published by Pebble,
1710 Roe Crest Drive, North Mankato, Minnesota 56003
www.mycapstone.com

Copyright © 2019 by Pebble, a Capstone imprint. All rights reserved. No part of this publication may be reproduced in whole or in part, or stored in a retrieval system, or transmitted in any form or by any means, electronic, mechanical, photocopying, recording, or otherwise, without written permission of the publisher.

Library of Congress Cataloging-in-Publication Data is available on the Library of Congress website.
ISBN 978-1-9771-0356-7 (library binding)
ISBN 978-1-9771-0526-4 (paperback)
ISBN 978-1-9771-0363-5 (ebook pdf)

Editorial Credits:
Anna Butzer, editor
Juliette Peters, designer
Tracy Cummins, media researcher
Kathy McColley, production specialist

Photo Credits:
Capstone: Eric Gohl, 9 Bottom, 11, 17 Top, 19; iStockphoto: Wilsilver77, 13 Bottom; Shutterstock: anthony heflin, 2–3, 20–21, Betty Shelton, 16 Bottom, 17 Middle, BlueBarronPhoto, 8, Christine Krahl, Design Element, Dave Allen Photography, Back Cover, Cover Top, Don Fink, 12 Top, ehrlif, 18–19, Gabbie Berry, 17 Bottom Left, gary718, 7, 22–23, 24–25, jadimages, 13 Top, 15 Bottom Left, Jerry Whaley, 10 Bottom, Jim Vallee, 5 Bottom, John Brueske, 14-15, John Wollwerth, 18 Bottom, Jon Bilous, 9 Top, Joshua Rozad, 3 Bottom, 15 Bottom Right, Kyle T Perry, 17 Bottom Right, Mark Baldwin, 1, Melinda Fawver, 15 Top, Nagel Photography, 3 Middle, NottomanV1, Design Element, outdoorimages, 4–5, Paul Winterman, Cover Bottom Right, Schwartz Nature Images, 3 Top, Shriram Patki, Cover Bottom Middle, 10–11, sstevens3, Cover Bottom Left, Steven Schremp, 6–7, topimages, 16 Top, Vlad Klok, Design Element, Wildnerdpix, 12 Bottom

Printed and bound in the USA.
1335

Table of Contents

Welcome to Great Smoky Mountains National Park

Great Smoky Mountains is the most visited national park in the United States. The park is in the Appalachian Mountains. Part of the park is in North Carolina. The other part is in Tennessee.

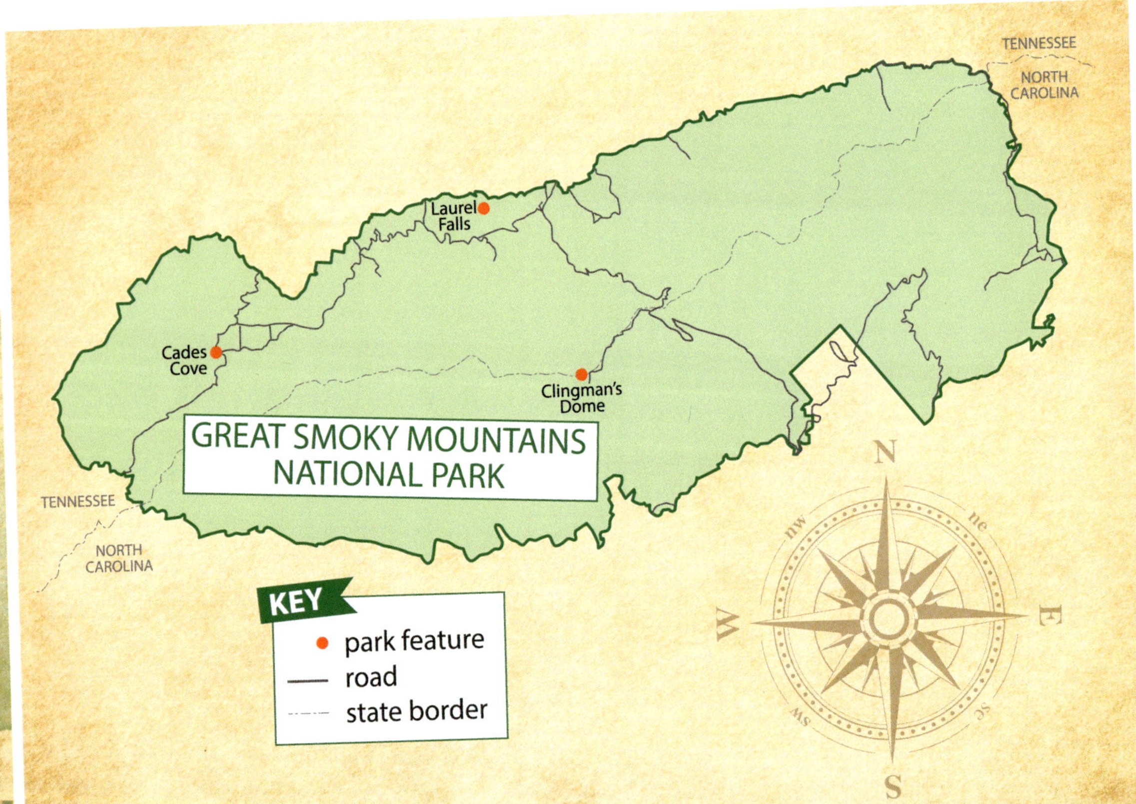

FACT: The park covers 816 square miles (2,113 square kilometers).

Great Smoky Mountains became a national park in 1934. People come from all over the world to see its thick forests and flowing streams.

Big Mountains

The Great Smoky Mountains are often covered with fog that looks like smoke. In fact, that is how the park got its name. The fog makes the mountains look blue and gray.

The mountains are about 270 million years old. Over time **erosion** caused them to have round tops.

erosion—wearing away of rock or soil by wind, water, or ice

^ observation tower

The highest spot in the park is Clingman's Dome. It is 6,643 feet (2,025 meters) tall. Visitors can climb to the top of the Dome on **paved** trails.

paved—when a road or sidewalk is covered with a hard material such as concrete or asphalt

At the top of the paved path is an observation tower. Visitors can see for 100 miles (161 km) in all directions from the top of the tower.

view from Clingman's Dome

Appalachian Trail – Clingman's Dome to Newfound Gap

N
E
S
W

Newfound Gap Road

Newfound Gap

Newfound Gap Road

Clingman's Dome Road

Tennessee

North Carolina

Clingman's Dome

KEY

- park feature
- Trail to Clingman's Dome
- Appalachian Trail
- road
- river
- visitor center
- state border

The Appalachian Trail stretches for 71 miles (114 km) in the park.

Hike to Laurel Falls

Visitors hike the Laurel Falls Trail to explore the forests that cover the mountains. The trail is about 4 miles (6.4 km) long roundtrip. **Evergreen** trees stand tall along the way.

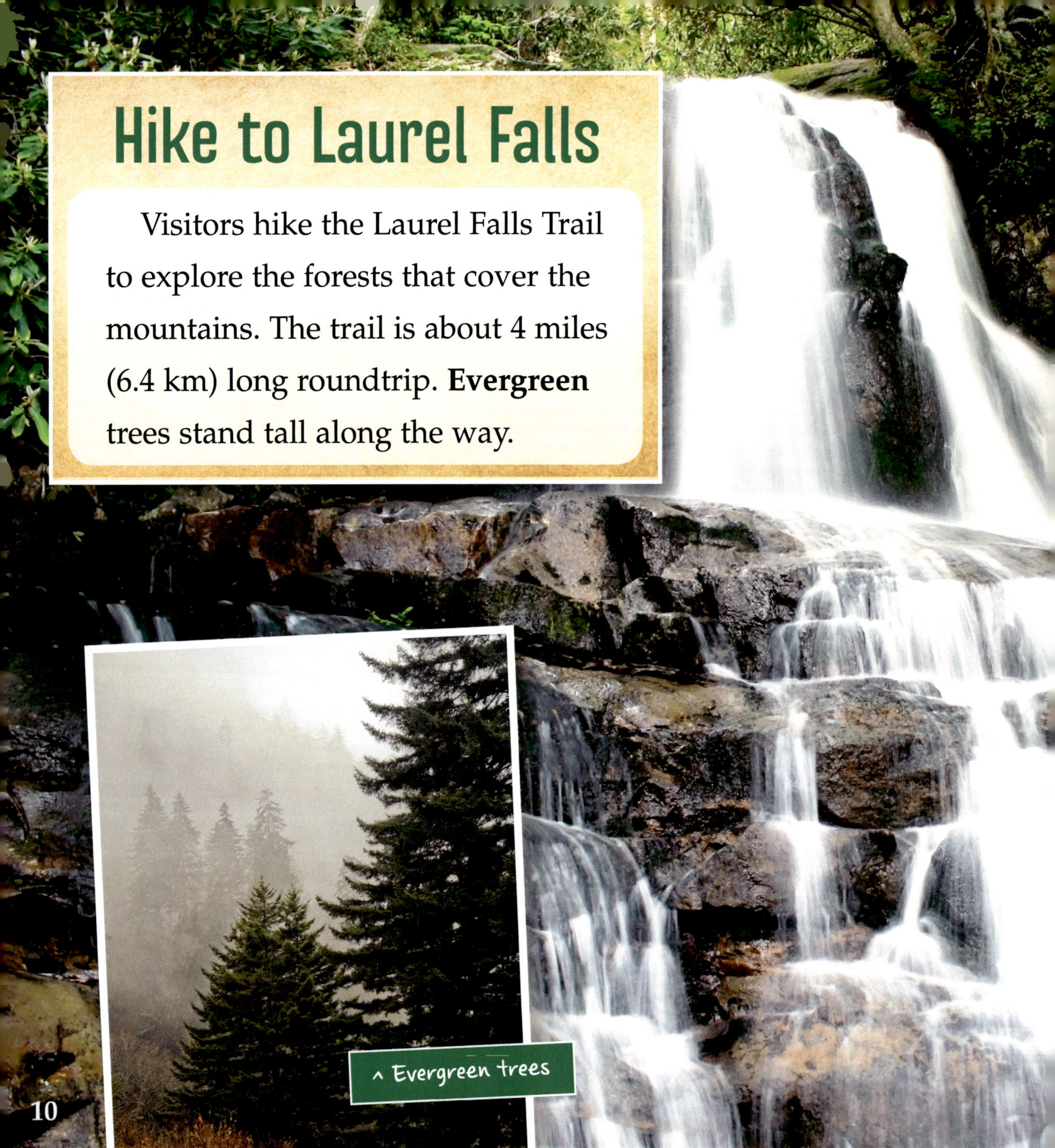

^ Evergreen trees

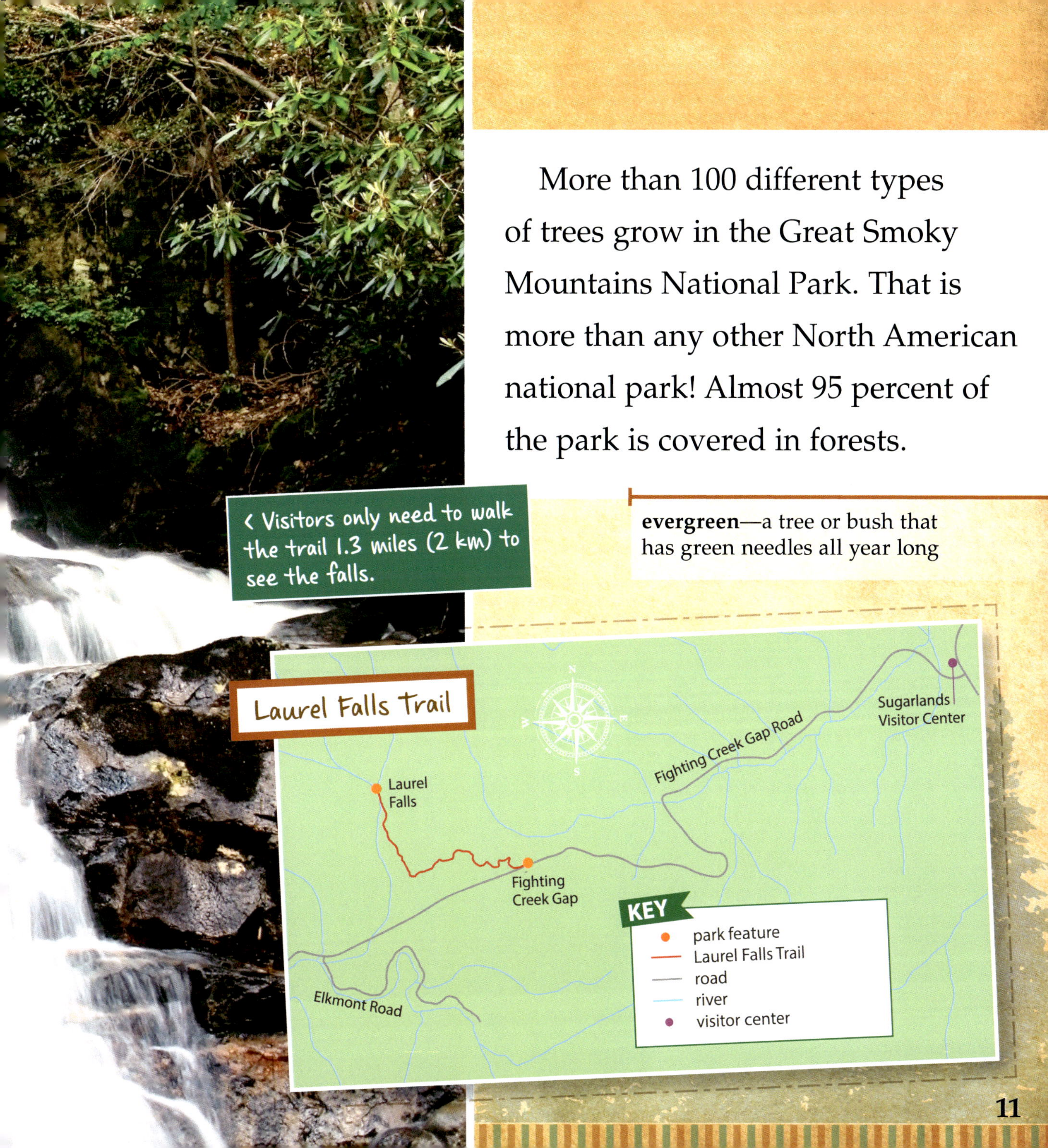

More than 100 different types of trees grow in the Great Smoky Mountains National Park. That is more than any other North American national park! Almost 95 percent of the park is covered in forests.

evergreen—a tree or bush that has green needles all year long

‹ Visitors only need to walk the trail 1.3 miles (2 km) to see the falls.

The trees in the park are big because it is in an **old-growth forest**. This type of forest has trees that are more than 100 years old.

old-growth forest—a natural forest that has grown over a long period of time

FACT: Laurel Falls gets its name from mountain laurel bushes. The bushes grow near the waterfall and along the trail.

The park is also home to wildlife, including bears. About 1,500 black bears live in the park. The park is the largest protected bear **habitat** in the world. Visitors might see deer, flying squirrels, and chipmunks too.

^ black bear

habitat—the natural place and conditions in which a plant or animal lives

^ The trail to Laurel Falls is paved. This is the most traveled path in the park.

Wonderful Wetlands

One of the easier hiking trails is the Fighting Creek Nature Trail. The trail is 1.4 miles (2.3 km) long. It passes through **wetlands**, so there are many streams and creeks.

^ red trillium

^ jack-in-the-pulpit

^ lady's slipper orchid

Many plants live in the wetlands. Some plants are wildflowers, such as red trillium, jack-in-the-pulpit, and lady's slipper orchids.

wetland—an area of land covered by water and plants; marshes, swamps, and bogs are wetlands

Ponds in the park are filled with frogs, salamanders, and other **amphibians**. Dragonflies and other insects fly over the water. Owls, hawks, and eagles fly over too. They are looking for lizards, mice, and other small animals to eat.

amphibian—a cold-blooded animal with a backbone; amphibians live in water when young and can live on land as adults

Fighting Creek Nature Trail

KEY
- Fighting Creek Trail
- road
- river
- visitor center

Park Headquarters Road
Newfound Gap Road
Fighting Creek Gap Road
Fighting Creek

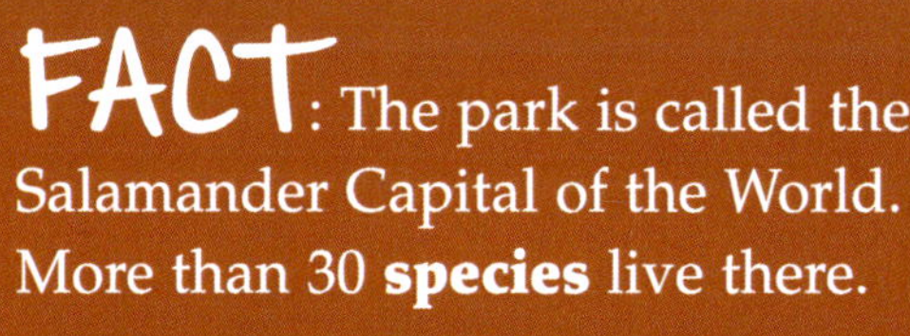

FACT: The park is called the Salamander Capital of the World. More than 30 **species** live there.

species—a group of animals with similar features

History Lives Here

Long ago some of the Great Smoky Mountains were home to the Cherokee Indians. They lived off the land. They hunted and fished. They grew corn and other foods. They made houses from reeds or wood.

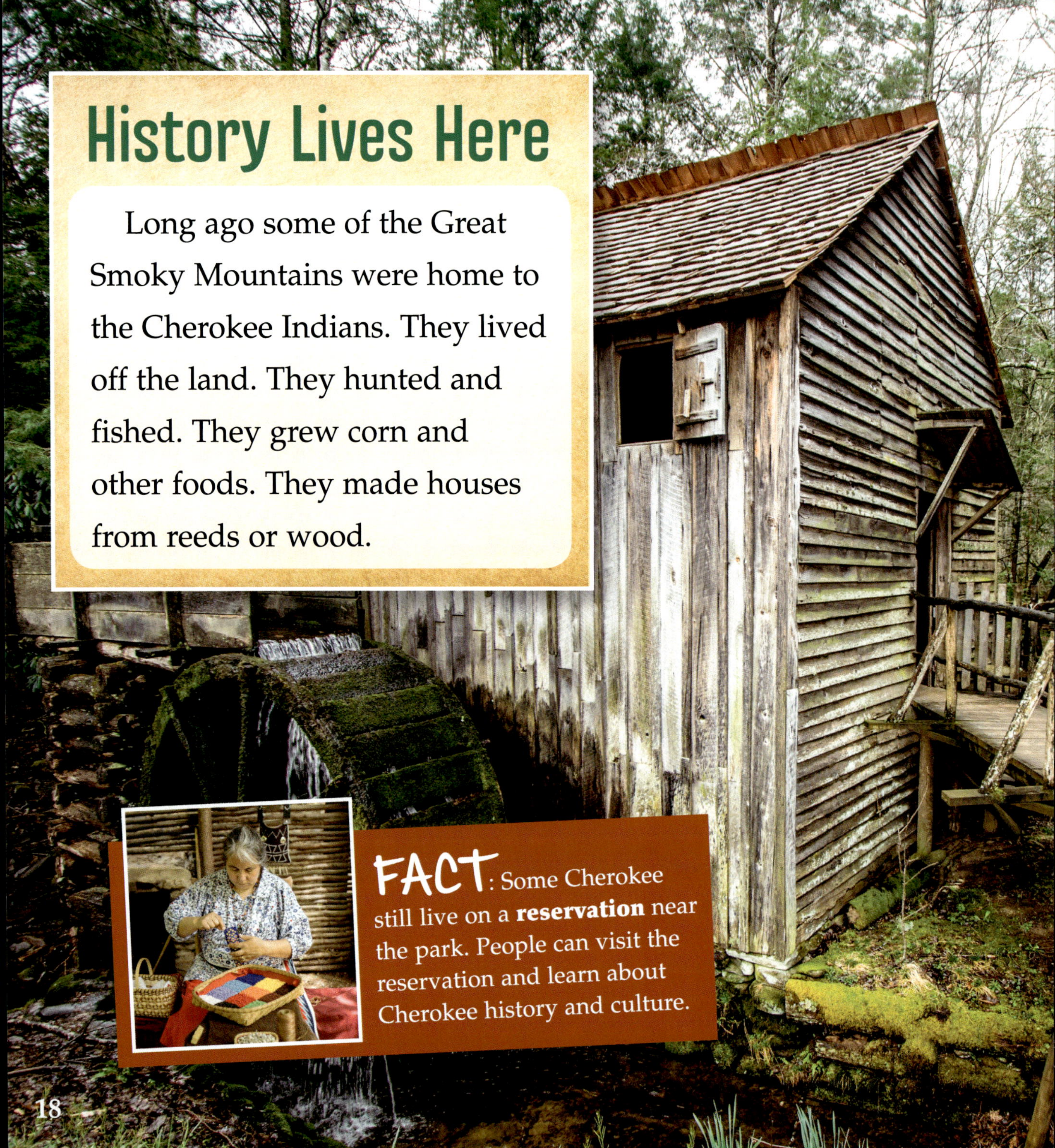

FACT: Some Cherokee still live on a **reservation** near the park. People can visit the reservation and learn about Cherokee history and culture.

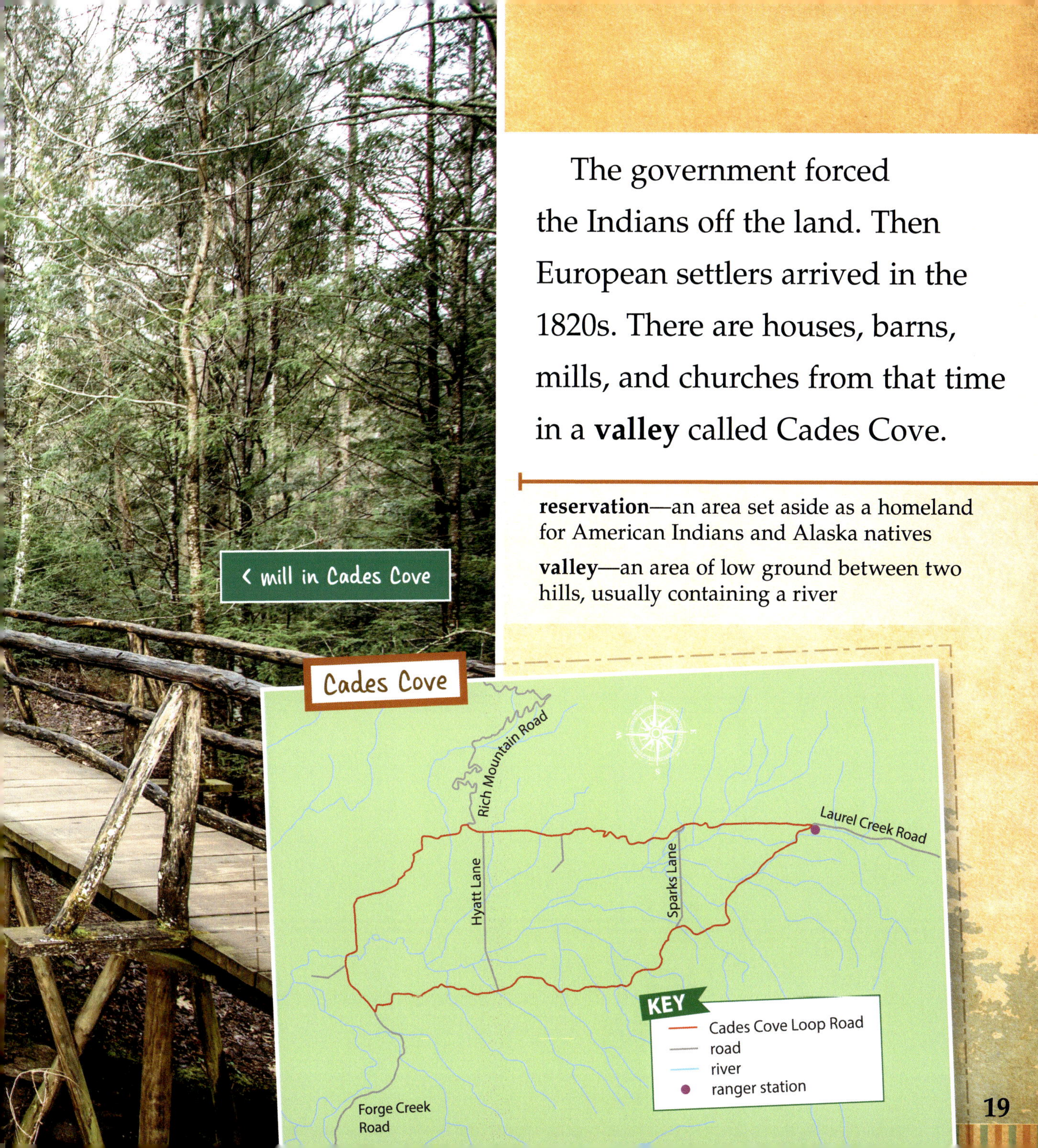

The government forced the Indians off the land. Then European settlers arrived in the 1820s. There are houses, barns, mills, and churches from that time in a **valley** called Cades Cove.

reservation—an area set aside as a homeland for American Indians and Alaska natives

valley—an area of low ground between two hills, usually containing a river

The settlers who lived in the park cut down many trees. Later on, large companies did the same. People worried that the Great Smoky Mountains were being destroyed. They asked the government to help. After many years, the government made it a national park to protect the land forever.

^ Newfound Gap overlook

Glossary

amphibian (am-FI-bee-uhn)—a cold-blooded animal with a backbone; amphibians live in water when young and can live on land as adults

erosion (i-ROH-zhuhn)—wearing away of rock or soil by wind, water, or ice

evergreen (E-vuhr-green)—a tree or bush that has green needles all year long

habitat (HAB-uh-tat)—the natural place and conditions in which a plant or animal lives

old-growth forest (old-GROHTH FOR-ist)—a natural forest that has grown over a long period of time; old-growth forests are more than 100 years old

paved (PAYVED)—when a road or sidewalk is covered with a hard material such as concrete or asphalt

reservation (rez-er-VAY-shuhn)—an area set aside as a homeland for American Indians and Alaska natives

species (SPEE-sheez)—a group of animals with similar features

valley (VAL-ee)—an area of low ground between two hills, usually containing a river

wetland (WET-land)—an area of land covered by water and plants; marshes, swamps, and bogs are wetlands

Read More

Herrington, Lisa. *Great Smoky Mountains National Park.* Rookie National Parks. New York: Scholastic, 2018.

Hunt, Santana. *Great Smoky Mountains National Park.* Road Trip: National Parks. New York: Gareth Stevens Publishing, 2016.

Spalding, Maddie. *Great Smoky Mountains National Park.* National Parks. Minneapolis: ABDO Publishing, 2017.

Internet Sites

Use FactHound to find Internet sites related to this book:

Visit *www.facthound.com*

Just type in 9781977103567 and go.

Check out projects, games and lots more at
www.capstonekids.com

Critical Thinking Questions

1. Why are national parks important parts of our country?

2. Describe amphibians. Use the text and the Glossary to help you.

3. What could you learn from visiting buildings like those found in Cades Cove?

Index